ORPHAN 2

Written By
Okello Oculi

Published by:
SYNTEL-AZA MEDIA PRODUCTIONS LTD
+234 806 555 0592

ISBN: 978-978-934-649-3

Copyright © **Okello Oculi** 2018

All rights reserved. This book is protected under the copyright laws of Nigeria. This book may not be copied or reprinted for commercial gain or profit, in any form or by any means, electronic or mechanical including photocopying, recording or by any information storage and retrieval system now known or here after invented, without the clear and express permission of the author.

Printed in Nigeria By:
Sn. Communications
+234 803 405 6570

Appreciation

This work is part of Africa Leadership Development Project

un a Rockefeller Foundation Fellowship at Bellagio Conference Centre, near Lake Como, Italy.

Preface

This work is anchored on an imagined drama of African diplomacy within and outside the corridors of Africa Hall, the seat of the African Union, successor to the Organisation of African Unity.

The Drama sketch in "Centre Stage" was acted out by students from Anglican Girls Grammar School (AGGS) Abuja, to the their peers as well as to an adult audience at an auditorium of Nigeria Labour Congress (NLC) on 8th November, 2016. The simulation event was a prelude to a lector by Professor Mwesiga Baregu of the University of Dar Es Salaam, Tanzania.

In 2006 and 2007, trained students from Makini Secondary School in Nairobi, Kenya and a team from AGGS undertook exchange travel and presented joint simulations of Summits of Heads of State of the African Union, rooted in research on each African country being represented, to audiences in Abuja and Nairobi, alternately.

The work hints at the vision of taking the politics and literary elements in pan-African diplomacy to the masses of the people. A growing body of criticism has targeted the monopolisation of African diplomacy by African heads of governments and their top bureaucratic officials and external consultants.

Severe comments have gone so far as to regard the situation as a "club' or "cabal" of self-indulgent leaders who do not report contents of their meetings to their respective country publics; as well as cover up each other's failures, including corruption and violations of people's rights.

SPIRIT OF ORPHAN

As the spirit of Orphan 2 walked across 54 clouds, she heard Girl-Heads of State of the African Union at a festival of eating these Word of politics.

PANA Correspondent:

"This is the Pan-African News Agency calling from Addis Ababa. Hello Dakar, Hello Tripoli, Hello Harare, Hello Johannesburg, Hello Lagos. The summit of the African Union is in session in AFRICA HALL.

Prime Minister Hailemarian Desaleign has had talks with President Uhuru Kenyatta of Kenya and Yoweri Museveni of Uganda over the 2015 elections in South Sudan.

President Macky Sall of Senegal is about to address the Summit. He may touch on the issue. Let us listen".

Press Conference

1. What are your views on President Obama's relations with Africa?

    He is only interested in our wild elephants while American companies exploit Africa. His Government agents have started wars in Mali, Central African Republic and South Sudan.

2. What is Zimbabwe's position in constructing the Ethiopian Renaissance dam?

    I am happy about it, it is a welcome one but Egypt must understand that the Nile waters are from rains that fall on Kenya, Rwanda, Tanzania Uganda and Ethiopia. The rain washes soils from these countries and has supported Egyptian agriculture for centuries.

    The Nile waters must be shared by all. They should not fall for the colonial, wicked plot of the British to cause conflict among African countries over the sharing of the Nile waters which is for the development of everyone.

Centre Stage

BOTSWANA

My delegation is glad to teach Africa our success in cutting our diamonds to make them good for export. Africa's First Ladies must be patriotic and buy beauty necklaces, earrings and rings from Botswana.

Dr Tajudeen Abdul-Raheem used to tell people "DO NOT AGONISE; ORGANIZE". He must have eaten OSTRICH EGGS in Gaborone and got that motto from our ANCESTORS!

My Government is concerned about children who do not

grow to their full height. They are STUNTED Children. It is because they eat very little food.

Some of the children may grow to become Heads of State and Governments...

TANZANIA
Objection President Chairperson!
Parents in BOTSWANA pull necks of their children for them to grow to be as tall as their OSTRICHES. It is VIOLENCE against children.

We must call for end to VISAS. Let Africans move freely across the continent. The 68 BILLION Dollars to be invested by businesses in Africa, as agreed at the WORLD ECONOMIC FORUM in Abuja must be done by JOINT efforts of workers who move freely across our borders.

East Africa will be investing in Nigeria. We may also train Nigerians how to run marathons.

SENEGAL
President Chairperson
Foreign boats are PLUNDERING our fish in Senegal's coastal waters. I am told that last year, 2013, they carried away fish of 1.3 BILLION American Dollars. Our women who market fish are now hungry. Our people are not eating well. Africa must join us in defending our fish from the rich coasts from Morocco to Namibia.

My delegation is presenting a Resolution to condemn politicians who become too fat when the people who voted for them are thin from hunger.

They are making people lose interest in elections. People are angrily calling 'BIG STOMACHS' as democracy
We are trying the SON of the former President in COURT for CORRUPTION.

Finally we have a fruit which makes a drink better than COCA COLA. It makes children do very well in school. Africa must listen to this news.

UGANDA

We want to advise Nigeria that there must be NO NEGOTIATIONS with terrorists. We Just KILL them.

That is how we defeated Joseph KONY in Uganda. We are now hunting for them in jungles of Central African Republic.

That is how we are defeating AL SHAABAB in Somalia.

If a politician becomes too fat it means he or she will die of heart attack and open the way for others. We should leave them to kill themselves.

I must warn Ghana, Madagascar, Niger, and Angola to tell the Chinese to refine oil in their countries; not carry crude thousands of kilometres away. Zambia and Congo should also refine their copper at home. That is what we are doing in Uganda.

Areas of interest of this MEETING or is it what you call SUMMIT ...We have only one on the top of Ruwenzori Mountain ... My delegation wants to spend our energies on things that matter to our people.

- Malaria
- Land robbed from villagers/small-scale farmers
- Corruption
- Returning CHIBONG GIRLS IN NIGERIA ALIVE

EGYPT

The Egyptian military did NOT do a COUP against President Mohammed Morsi.

Egyptians from many political ideas voted for him to be the first democratically elected leader since military rule in 1952.
But he betrayed their trust when he started to rule according to SHARIA LAW as the Muslim Brotherhood directed him.
The angry voters stayed in the streets PLEADING with the MILITARY to save the nation from civil war.
We heard the voice of 15 million EGYPTIANS voting by DEMONSTRATIONS.
We heard the wishes of a people. We only answered our duty as PATRIOTS.

The African Union must end keeping Egypt outside your meetings.

KENYA
President Chairperson
Egyptian soldiers KILLED over ONE THOUSAND demonstrators who were standing with President MORSI.

You crushed them under military tanks. That is what the world saw on television.

You killed FATHERS of CHILDREN; DAUGHTERS and SONS.
You must be tried in an African court.
When white policemen and soldiers in racist South Africa murdered children in SOWETO, Africa fought them.
My Government will try you in our court if the African Union agrees.

AU COMMISSION CHAIR (Dr. Nkosazana Dlamini-Zuma)
We congratulate Nigeria for reducing money spent for buying food from other countries by 5 BILLION Dollars in 2013

We congratulate China's Prime Minister for visiting the AU Secretariat in Addis Ababa; visiting Ethiopia, Nigeria, Angola and Lenya. In Nigeria he made a speech at the WORLD ECONOMIC FORUM AFRICA in Abuja, Nigeria.

He made a promise to spend 30 Billion Dollars in Africa in the future..

Last year China and Nigeria traded together for a total of 13.5 million Dollars

China must bring investment into Africa but employ more local people in the construction works in Africa such as building a new housing village outside of Luanda in Angola; a railway line from Kaduna to Abuja in Nigeria; an electric railway in Addis Ababa and roads in Kenya.

We encourage and congratulate Ethiopians for working on the ETHIOPIAN RENAISSANCE DAM. It is to produce 6,000 megawatts of electricity at the cost of 4 BILLION US Dollars. It is being built by 8,000 workers working day and night.
We thank NIGERIA for hosting a successful WORLD ECONOMIC FORUM. We saw that top business leaders from Africa and Presidents of RWANDA, GHANA, TANZANIA, KENYA and Prime Ministers of Mali and Niger came to Abuja to be at the meeting. They showed that fear of terrorism will not be allowed to stop Africa travelling on the road to development.

INSIGHTS

Voice 1: Our African ancestors know when to laugh. Imagine them chasing that sharp faced boy, Andry Rajoelina, to be the mushroom sprout as the spirit of Barrack Obama sitting on water. Did you hear his hunger: "There must be no power Vacuum".

Voice 2: Why waste more time on Kenya. Mau Mau blood only fertilizes Luo and Kikuyu corruption in that land.

Voice 3: Marc Ravalomanana is still crying at waves to bring his love back to him.

Voice 1: Island people know how to run away from sea waves chasing at their heels.

Voice 2: Their people are starving while old European men bored with their wealthy living come to Madagascar to buy sex from little girls eleven years old.

Voice 3: Their wasted blood returns from coasts in Peru and Indonesia chanting as mass madness.

Voice 1: This time our ancestors want to wash Africa with Obama's song of change. When his grandmother went on the eve of his election we should have known that corruption all across Africa would suffer "heavy manners" (as Bob Marley would scream).

Voice 2: When you hear that Nigerians too are fighting corruption, the "End Time" is near (laughing). Did you hear that story? When a ten-year old Hausa boy was asked what he wants to be when he grows up, he answered "Gwamna" (Governor). Why? "Ina so Kudi" (I want money), he said, smiles in his two eyes.

Voice 2: Those Nigerians have turned to women to wash corruption off their bottoms; and their women look so tough!

Voice 3: Why not, with all the pepper they eat. Their stomachs send fire inside heads of babies in their wombs.

Voice 1: So that is where all their madness comes from – what they call "bad belle"!

Voice 2: What is inside those fat Zulu women?

Voice 3: Mandela's screams calling Chaka! – for a boxing fight.

PEER REVIEW

Cameroun:
President Mugabe,
you have been in power since 1980;
spent 20 years laughing
with a wife who is fourty years younger
than your junior sister.

Mugabe:
Mr President
why are you paying salaries
of officials in your Foreign Ministry?
Come for adult literary lessons
in Zimbabwe's history.
When in 1979 we were winning
the liberation war
against your white ancestors,
those in Britain, America, France
and Scandinavia eating our
country
shouted at our brothers Samora Machel
of Mozambique,
Mwalimu Nyerere
of Tanzania
father of all liberation and freedom wars
in Southern Africa
God's Head Angel in "After-Africa",
General Obasanjo as Nigeria's military bulldozer:

they sat pressure on them
to intimidate us in ZANU-Patriotic Front
to carry an empty basket of independence
leaving behind all our land
in rotten stomachs of white farmers.
They said 1980 to 1990 must wear my silence
keep quiet
just be looking like a blind
snake tongue flicking, groping
at white people laughing their
rotten teeth at our people for
fighting and dying
to remain poor and landless.
When 1990 arrived Kaunda
and Obasanjo came
begged me not to take back our land
avoid frightening white land robbers in South Africa
and Namibia
and pop Mandela out of prison
take soup of power to African National
Congress a taste of eating from their land. We
heard their heart.
We did not seize land.

Senegal
Mr Mugabe,
in my country
we pay people to tell us stories.
call them "griots":

keepers of our memory.
They recite our family histories
using sweet voices in drums
and Cora melodies.
But they are not elected presidents
or chiefs
because rulers must take action
not feed people with empty air
from their empty mouths.
Perhaps you will like to leave Zimbabwe
and come to sing
tell stories of your ancestors
about corruption in your government.
Without fear of doubt
swoon of the little girl you call your wife
owner of 2 large eyes and 4 large farms;
land grabbed for all your ministers of Cabinet ....

Mugabe
Mr Brother President, you
may shut your mouth
help the Ozone Layer.

Guinea Bissau
Brother Mugabe,
that reality that your wife commandeers
pilots AIR ZIMBABWE that metal
buzzing fly
carrying wives of party officials and ministers
for shopping in Gadafi's Tripoli;

King of fashionable boutiques
And nuclear bombs powerful un-exploded;
Billowing whims of women who yesterday
were wearing cloth their husbands used as blankets,
wilting moral authority with our people.

Mugabe
Comrade Samora Machel
used to say to us
you cannot hold up the
sky with one finger.
Use a fist made of 5 strong fingers.
The white settlers we are fighting
own vast tracks of land in one finger;
own banks in finger 2;
own trading companies as finger 3.
They used terror as finger 4 to declare "ownership".
That smell of our soil,

Dews in our bushes and chests of our mountain;
Roars, bellows and sneezes of our wild animals
Longed for without fruit in Europe
which they know cannot hug them in Europe
is finger 5,
and makes them fight us
with wild ferocity.
If I must defeat them
I must fight them with black Zimbabweans
who also know the use of bullet power;
Zimbabweans who talk of freedom

and independence in their cows mooing,
hear factories belching their name; hear
rattles of dollars in our ambitions.
Healing those taught to be deaf;
learnt nonsense, never peered through fog
of Europe building its power by selling
and planting sorrows of their people and our peoples.
My brothers,
the whites in Zimbabwe,
eat terror at my being successful
in being clean from corruption
raising Zimbabweans who know
the game of creating wealth, and
using the gun ;
our army pointing guns at them ....

GABON (Omar Bongo)
Mr Mugabe, your Excellency. Thief,
a political thief is a thief whether he
be born white or black.
Your government robs excellent farmers
For being white
Ignoring past decades of their maize
fed your own black labourers
who gave their genius and sweat
to global civilization
in gold and diamond out of mines in South Africa,
herding cattle of South-West Africa (now Namibia),
weeding and harvesting farms of Southern Rhodesia

(now Zambia).

A small number
only 6,000 white farmers
yielded annual miracles in our tropics.
Now, you rob them of their historic responsibility
throwing their mission to army generals, bush
guerrilla fighters
who ravaged wild fruits and roots and
leaves hostile to digestion
even to their wild and furious bellies
never known about crop rotation;
party fanatics
carrying farming inside their fat stomachs
leaving land looted for them to lie idle
indifferent as free livestock
that in wise hands raised milk
and beef
which travelled as far north as our
supermarkets. Your cronies run fish ponds by
holding picnics, in drunken revelries
roast and gulp up fish that should be laying eggs.
Forgive my peaking with much wrath, heat and
despair.
4 million of your people are starving.
Swaziland and Lesotho, your abandoned neighbours,
Exist with calamity
drought has eaten food crops.

You must be responsible in the spirit of
African brotherhood.

Amilcar Cabral
Mr Presidential, houseboy of France.
You talk of political thieves.
Talk also of Executive and Presidential stupidity
and inept treason.
The land of Zimbabwe is our ancestral
heritage and not that of Europe
armed robbers of1890, 1910 or 2004.
Screams in hysteria by Radio France,
Voice of America,
the BBC and satellite mouths in Gabon
do not wash away furies of white murderers
guns in slaughters
and loot of orphaned herds of cattle
filling horizons in thought. Their
telling you lies;
that Mugabe is bullying European
gangsters should be a tonic, a bile
waking that waiting manhood in you.
Aluta Continua looks for victory.

South Africa
Mr President of Ethiopia,
they tell me of a company
called MIDROC INTERNATIONAL:
doing all the construction work in your
country; roads;

used 350 million American dollars
to sprout SHERATON ADDIS hotel.
Luring a brother President
Who, trekking from borrowing new
loans seduced a "presidential suit"
at five thousand dollars per night.
In the spirit of Pan-Africanism
open to world-class construction companies
from South Africa.
Ethiopia gallantly joined our felling
ferocious crocodiles of racism in Southern Africa.
Fed our ending racism,
its not yielding poverty
and unemployment for blacks reading our skies.

ETHIOPIA
Brother Mbeki,
I am pleased that the businessman
Owner of this company is a wild
flower
 son of an Ethiopian womb of a woman.
Deep feelings of ancestry blow his banners.
The very high standards in this hotel lifts
its tribal marks to call as a "SPECIAL COLLECTION";
one in a clan of 117 existing in Africa –so far.

MALI
Mr President of Ethiopia.
It must be true that this special quality
also marks its location amid a forest of mass starvation;

buying off slums around her eyelashes
turning them to a green belt saving
her opulent suitors from
perfume of sweat and hunger of the people.
We know that winds in our Sahara Churn
arid hunger of Tuaregs to gunpowder.

Ethiopia
Mr President of Senegambia,
we in the new Ethiopia born
from a protracted war against
feudal military atrocities
swing "development" as swords for terminating ills
poverty and squalor
as normal clothes and vision of our people.
This seed of Ethiopia also bought SHERATON
Hotel in Kampala, Uganda,
investing a bribe of one million American dollars:
familiar green shade of banana leaves
in our Equator.

Mozambique
Mr President of Ethiopia.
My delegation joins our comrades from Eritrea
delighted that we no longer speak of "Emperor"
thrower of political cobras as breakfast for lions
or wise crocodiles.
That truly is "development".
We, yet, worry that your revolution

Swings her foliage as lurid invitation
to Arab billionaires in armouries of decadence

sojourning to Addis Ababa
to buy the sex of Ethiopian women,
some with beauties of Zulu women in dance of
liberation
and Mandingo women singing
to Futa Toro mountains of Guinea.
Tourism as cover for state-prostitution
Trafficking flesh on fire;
Grabbing Oromia geography of aspirations
willing investment in fires in the horizon.

Ghana
Mr President of Ethiopia.
I am a proud beneficiary of visionary importance
Kwame Nkrumah gave to sowing seeds of alphabets
into heads of our people
in all regions
access to schools as water wells of education
Governments of North Atlantic Treaty Organization
(NATO)
froathed in fright
At his sending out thousands of youth to
graze on trades of carpentry, tailoring,
Masonry and painting walls,
motor mechanics and weaving imagination
in East Germany,

in Poland and Russia
and Hungary
learning communism as freedom of talents
rolling out wings waxed by empire
run on bile and spite of victims not on three legs.
They escaped grovelling for degrees in Laws In
Engineering and arithmetic
Without tracing footprints to their ancestral
Geometry and Algebra in Ancient Egypt's pyramids;
Escaping prison of students blind to repairing broken
vehicles.

NATO went berserk hurling assassinations at
Nkrumah
Salivating at stopping him
breeding those with furnaces in hearts and minds
to manufacture machines. My delegation must
salute
President Meles Zenawe
for sowing seeds of light across
rumbling darkness that was Ethiopia.

Benin
We salute the good recalling of
Comrade Kwame Nkrumah; recall
loot of his papers and archives
American agents were allowed to loot
and scatter his documents on streets of Accra;
Illiterate soldiers in Ghana
Innocent in blindness of wisdom of world Socialism

danced for a freedom of idiocy;
as their European and American masters laughed
delirious in celebration and mockery of their
freed treason against Africa.
We must regret reports that
in 2001 only 20 per cent of children
across Southern Africa
who sat for Ordinary Level examinations passed;
80 per cent failed.
Two ministers of education
And the entire staff of the Education
Ministry Were proudly part of the 80 per
cent who Enjoyed those freedoms to fail.

Malawi

My embassy in Cotonou tell
of an annual increase of 20 per cent in importation
of alcohol and French frog-legs – not whole frogs –
as animation for their Socialist liberation from
revolution in tropical Africa.
A little bit of enjoyment keeps colonialism away.
President Laurent Gbagbo
Mr Chairman, Cote d'Ivoir advocates
the high lights of justice and equity
in our international actions.
We salute and endorse the goodwill and
responsibility Shed from Nigeria n Liberia and Sierra
Leone and Sao Tome.
Countries rich in diamonds, bauxite, aluminium and
even oil,

like a woman wearing fine jewellery,
lure people good and greedy alike.
We shine a glorious history of accommodating
our brothers and sisters from Mali, Guinea
and Niger,
Nigeria and Ghana and even the Sahara.
This too is a social, cultural diamond;
Hinting at love and blood hidden in voracious
diplomacy.
In our moments of civil conflict we require,
indeed we deserve equity through material support.
If Nigeria can bleed for Liberia and Sierra Leone –
and leaving behind a quarter of a million Nigerio-
Liberio babies ....

Nigeria
Before I let your wish picks our pocket,
let me speak a historic seriousness.
I believe that it is time we went back to
our pre-colonial generosity of villages and neighbours.
We in Nigeria walk with 36 feet;
cutting up the same bull elephant into smaller
and tiny pieces for our pots.
We should be increasing the size
and number of elephants:
by inviting Benin, Togo, Chad, Niger, Cote d'Ivoir
and solitude in our vast Sahara sands
ever blowing aspirations of harmattan particles of
dust,

to join us,
tango in Fela's Shakara tunes
in a common festival of nationhood.
Nigeria and Cameroun end cutting up strips of land
be talking, and talking
and talking
about a growing federal constitution
branded with hot palm oil;
that eats up colonial boundaries;
and the arrogance of racial and religious bigotry
of the Sahara.
Having said that,
May God and Allah and our Ancestors
Hear my fears that riotous Nigeria's media
will "pieces me' 'to "suya" – not for eating but
for spitting out.
Mr Chairman, if the President of Cote d'Ivoir
shall indulge a flare for tourism,
he should come and attend a meeting
of Nigeria's 36 governors snarling for
a share of the national revenue.

Zambia
Mr President Chairman,
talking of Nigeria's international actions –
some of which must be commended by Africans
worldwide –
I find it shameful that President General Sani Abacha
and his Vice President Fela Kuti

and her top businessmen
park private planes at Nairobi
airport to host drunken parties,
and hide stolen money in Kenyan banks.
This infection of Africa
spreads Nigeria's corruption and patriotism of looting.

Nigeria
Mr President Chairman,
let me inform that
we have just launched the National
OPEN UNIVERSITY
with a registration of 400,000 students
who study from their homes and bushes.
Our Federal Executive Council (or Cabinet as some of
you call it),
will be glad to pay fees of African leaders
who may wish to do a course on Nigeria's
history and administration.
Vice President Fela Kuti was elected to office in Africa
in 1987.
Perhaps we should open our meeting with a quiz
about affairs in our countries.
Those who score 70 per cent failure must attend
lessons,
while others are meeting.
I fail to see how Presidential ignorance about
African and world affairs
is not a disgraceful form of corruption;
and escapes inclusion in illiteracy statistical scores.

Gambia

One thing over which there is no ignorance
is the horrible arithmetic that 150 women in
Nigeria die daily while giving life at birth. Some
people claim, in ridicule,
that Gambian military officers learnt
the art of conducting the 1974 military
coup from attending a military academy in
Kaduna, Nigeria.
The fact that Nigerians eat groundnuts
does not mean that they learnt to ingest its merits
from Gambia and Senegal.
And any of you want to be toilet cleaners in
Banjul Make sure your nose does not bleed;
And your legs can haul you away in fright.

Thomas Sankara

A wise poet in India has
said that the biggest disease
which afflicts women the world over
is silence, more silence and still more silence
about the sufferings of women.
We must fight revolutions inside brains of Africans.
Our women must learn to talk, and talk and talk

till they dissolve putrid prejudices and blindness
inside minds of men;
especially feudal parasitical men; our Chiefs.

Those that cover their evil murders by poison

against their rival
by making widows drink waste water
from washed bodies of dead husbands
must be whipped by teams of women.
Universal education for female children
will free their inventive geniuses
for Africa's industrial and artistic development.

Namibia

Odd political murders hit Nigeria:
that of Chief Bola Ige (of the Alliance for Democracy),
Chief Harry Marshal (of All Nigeria Peoples Party)
fell,
and Chief Aminosoari of the Peoples Democratic
Party) met
mood of rivalry,
we warned of borrowed America's constitution
wearing
casual celebration of gun murders.
Many Nigerians come to our country,
some disguised as footballers plotting
to cheat our border and whims of South Africa.
Perhaps soon guns will come with them; guns!;
instead of seeds of grass
to tame tempers of our Kalahari desert
so that it can yield happiness of stomachs,
not tears of childless virginity.

Chad

I see that the President of Uganda was shaking his head

Hearing of security hiding in Namibia's President
talking of cross-border brotherhood. Since Idi
Amin fled
galaxy of military medals jangling from his chest,
more peoples have died from guns.
He should worry not of Nigerian guns
crossing Central African Republic and
Congo to drink blood in Uganda.
Those clinging to his history
should gun down old age,
cheeky hands of senility
and the compulsory exit
from the Departure Hall
of the flight to After-Africa.
We in Chad always told Hissen Habre,
The Grand Locust,
that in the affairs of politics,
sands in the Sahara will always have the last laugh.

Uganda
Mr Chairman President,
I am a revolutionary.
Revolutionaries feed on hearing feelings
and thoughts of the people
because that is the bull they rode on,
guns blazing,
to eat power;
cook change.
The people of Uganda always elect me.
That is that.

Guns as a tongue of dialogue
is decimating feetless populations in South Sudan.

Not used to people voting for them, Her
leaders never known of community:
killing as voting for them, loyalty as
farming blood.
If populations of ethnic nationalities are unequal
it is stupid to run government on subtraction,
killing others as weeds.
Uganda will not allow Arabs to fish
on the source of the Nile leaving
South Sudanese as weeds bleeding
in long *fadama* farms; silted refugee
camps inside Uganda.

 Eritrea
Some World Bank officials told of Uganda
distributing guns to KARIMOJONG people in their
northeast
and paid them monthly wages
to prospect for gold
guns killing ethnic others who wear gold
in their graves
reside on land with gold mines first
dug by British colonial officials and
South African companies.
We know that is not good governing.
That is a return to ways of colonial wars,

white imperialists hating us,
loving our mineral resources.

Uganda
Mr Chairman President,
let me ask the President of Eritrea
which colonial officials sent him
to kill innocent Ethiopians in a stupid war
over rocky patches of land,
even fallen soldiers not tasting soil.
We honour his people defeating
a stupid army of Emperor Haile
Selassie after a 30 year-War.
We commend protecting the gold,
diamonds and other minerals in his country
from greedy imperialists.
If he needs our help, we must offer it, freely.
What we know is that brains of the people
are superior to minerals under soils in our countries.
Let us not spill them with useless wars; and
megalomania.

Mozambique
The Commission wishes that we break for lunch.
We propose that delegates walk
through Africa HALL OF FREEDOM
and observe an excellent exhibition
of photographs organized by the inspiration
of Ambassador Segun Olusola,

Nigeria's former envoy to Ethiopia.
See a lesson in another smile.

Rwanda
Mr Chair President,
Chairperson of African Union Commission, Dr.
Nkosazana Dlamini-Zuma . My delegation rejects
this plea,
Viewing horrible photographs of death,
starvation among Africa's refugees
will murder appetites of your Excellencies,
high Presidents and Heads of State. With
sorrow in their hearts,
the leaders will not enjoy the official banquet.
These same excellencies remained silent;
went to shop in Tokyo,
scrambled in Geneva and New York
for new shoes,
flowing silk gowns and false
teeth for their wives
while genocide rolled its appetite
through Rwanda's towns,
drowned villages and desecrated churches.
They should not shed tears of sand here.

D.R.Congo
Mr President Chair,
the delegation of the glorious
and revolutionary Democratic Republic of
Congo will raise the matter of reparations

for those, with Rwanda,
turned eastern frontiers of our
country into a death jungle
for over 5 million of Congolese villagers,
teachers, doctors
school children
between 1998 to 2016.
Barbaric rape of our women was alien to us
Seizing lands containing rare mineral resources;
drinking the blood of Congolese
is never a communion for moral
and dignified good power.

Mali
Mali proposes that we formally salute,
Tunisia, Gabon and Equatorial Guinea
for organizing football festivals for our youth
– both women and men.
We must congratulate Carthage Eagles of Tunisia,
Eagles of Cote d'Ivoir
for winning under whispers of Bourghiba
and Houphuet Boigny
We, of course, invite you to celebrate the four goals
scored by a Malian star and patriot, KUNONTE,
and patriotic Drogba.
We must droop our hearts
In salute to Coach Stephen Keshi of Nigeria;
Demonstrator of calm capacity of an African coach
reaching highest levels of football: his eyes on
World Cup warriorhood.

Liberia
We must never overlook the deliberate
failure by Tunisia's official
to honour Nigeria's National Anthem
during the ceremony for the game between
Nigeria and Tunisia.
As people who benefited from the honour
of Nigeria's nationhood invested in Liberia
shedding of the blood of Nigeria's soldiers in our
land, we must to register our disgust and protest.
We shall venerate them
in our labours of renaissance;

build our diplomacy on farm
ploughs pulled by our timber,
our weeping rubber trees
lamenting roads not walked;
our aluminium,
and carving knives in brains of our youths.
Those who sent Ebola virus
to decimate our triumphant people,
and punish Nigeria, our redeemer, have failed.
We are a land of freedom for all, Never
looking back
Sweeping away cumulus clouds
Walking waves of our Atlantic Ocean
in our memories.

Algeria
If Charles Taylor had allowed Liberia's children

to play with football ,
not with guns,
perhaps you would be doing greater honour
to Nigeria's blood by not inviting it to be
wasted on your soil.
We fought a war of liberation,
not against ourselves;
honoured rage in our people till,
with sunsets at our earlobes,
wax grew across windows in our souls;
forgetting to hear electric waves in
breaths of Algerians:
farmers and mechanics,
and cobblers
and singers in markets;

irritation in tongues of women.
That is when those who whisper to Allah
through desert mist at dawn
threw curses against our words.
Noting folds in pages under our chins,
Mounds on backs on necks and waists
Of party officials and military keepers of gates
To belches, new believers
Blasted bones hiding indolence under uniforms.
Beware of fury in orphans.

Cote d'Ivoir(Quattara)
My delegation proposes a toast in RED wine
to celebrate gallant youth of Africa

on the Continent and in the Diaspora –
our spirit circulating as fertilizes of
human conscience.
That includes our own Laurent Gbagbo,
Now pardoned by victims of our politics
of arrogance and patriotism with broken teeth.

Tanzania

May be the president of Cote d'Ivoir should use
BLACK wine.
It will stop that hunger for vengeance in his country.
His Big Watchers broke bones, spilt ethnic pots of
hope.
Mwalimu was from a people filling a mere
village but grew into a vast territory Dropping
laughter
little bits of sugar into wits
with each Word,
Sacks of parables hauled on rough roads
Ploughing hearts in market crowds
Undoing wailings caked on footprints of marauding
German
Soldiers in flight from other empires:

Planting farms of famine.
His politics fed a familyhood
Lit flames of dignity, service to justice
ever mocking our bending to temptations
towards waving banners of selfishness.
He held hands with Houphuet Boigny

breaking legs in Africa's march to Union power
in 1963. Horns of men eating power would gore him;
unto weeping his error, filling the Indian Ocean. Join
us in healing the wounded star of Africa.

Kenya
I saw a report that after Mali lost to Morocco,
commentators in Tunisia did say:
"there goes the last of the last Africans";
Splashing mud at an Africa NATIONS CUP.
This is racism in sports.
Our HARAAMBEE STARS of Kenya
went to TUNISIA 2004 in the spirit of pan-Africanism;
for whose flowering Jomo Kenyatta gave his youth;
marrying an English woman as colonial revenge.

In the spirit of his footprints
We raise guns to silence new quarrels
that derail keeping our eyes
on wrath for land and stomach justice,
for which men died in guns for land;
women walked loaves of bread
pregnant with crouching pistols
waiting for touch of Mau-Mau warriors.

AFRICA TALKING

I have seen things
And things have eaten me
Washed my eyes with sun and dark.
Three cooking stones
Were too few for three
elephants With pots on banks of
water on a journey;
Pouring soups at each other,
yelling
steaming
boiling seedlings of a nation.

Grandmothers sat pots
with a triangle
to feed families
clans and people.

In Kenya three
Pots of Embu
Meru
Gikuyu
Are accused of cooking peas for each;
pebbles for others.
In Togo
To be near Sahara fire
is to eat all the meat.

In Nigeria three pots
Throw pepper soup across borders
to spite each other: Children
starving, play
in shadows waiting
for love of a flag.

In Zambia and Uganda
Ghana and Nigeria
 men of enterprise
fear leaking sweat on soil, grass and crops:
from dawn
mid of sun
knowing shadows of night
swooning on grasping moist hands of white
hunters in forests of lush tropical laziness
and embroidered sovereignty;
Men and wives poisoning
children
with chemical cheese-cake and green wine;
Ever commanding God to work overtime
giving them new bellies and hearts
Livers holding clandestine politics of graft
bowels inherited from elephants
Hosting legacies of nonsense and grasses.

In Kinshasa, lip of River Congo,
Children of Kongo Empire
Fed on salted footprints of 1210

Are tired of nomadic eyes from Kisangani
Rain-drenched toes from Kivu and Katanga
Kicking dust into their soup pots
Growl with Kibangui's pencil sketches on clouds,
Fancy fashion attires on slum stars
And blood on broken bottles of wrath
Shaving head of arrogance of exclusion from power;
Demanding hug of nationhood.

In Zimbabwe
Shona dirges to white ghosts fat on eating soils
And grasses
On hanging their youth by strings
As picnic fun,
Yearn to hear birds whip wings in clouds over hills,
Sit on twigs in their bushes and trees
 chirping, quacking and cooing;
And see wild mushroom swell
In their hands unto leaves of dollars;
to silence a thirst for feeding cubs of history.
It must come to come, as time is time.

In Ethiopia
Oromia splash their language to
water Stomping feet rumbling
in drunken gulp of raw arithmetic of power
long sleeping
bleeding under rusting imperial festivals.
Tigrinya keepers of gates to justice tremble and stumble

on roads to village hearts:
waiting for lessons from Malagasy youths wrestling
with bulls
without falling to sowing blood

In Nigeria
Korean, and Japanese and Qatari and Chinese tourists
Walk on oil spills
balancing on anthropology:
checking old note books of Euro-American oil sisters
for herbal vaccines
in harvesting hunger for adoration
flapping in flags over households;
tracking worshipers in shrines of 'I Before Nation'
watching out for outbreaks
of fires from free flows of greed,
and selling air to the poor.
An ancient will for hugging dignity of
household waits
knowing that dark rain clouds will clear and sunshine
shall
find soil or creek water with their eyes open;
that development shall come.

In Botswana and Lesotho
land of rivers of men selling lungs
to mine owners at Kimberley,
were joined by muscles traded from
Tanganyika and Malawi and Angola drowned
babies in testicles

as wombs of women
bubbled each moonlight
in homes hollowed of men
to pant at hoes sinking into wet soils,
banning cries of babies at birth
under hands of mothers blocking noses with bathing,
water of love tying mother to baby Dr Death

awoke mouths churning resolves for
reparations for years of this wet genocide until
Mandela walked again
hawking love as medication for small pox on History;
preaching welding elbows with juices of education;
spreading humus for talents
In Wolof and Fur and Chaga and Herero
And Khoi San and Zande and Soninke and Nyoro
Doctors sweating skill
of nano-mechanics on human arteries in brains
feeding faith in one people: dredging our
geography of orphans.

They say with glee: "thirst is Africa, rotting"
We retort: Africa is watching
those picking their teeth,
weaving her laughter Like
time
Shining eyes of History
as lionesses desecrate beauty in Zebras
hyenas giggle over elegant leaps in deers

and pythons slyly hug screaming jackals
in the name of life chewing life Creation
weeding her horizon
Weaving beats and cornrows on dance of landscapes

The rumble of her youth is foretold
 in their stepping
Jumping laughter
 of girls playing cheekying
lighting fires in tempers waving impatience
stoking hope and love in a species

They chant of Lagos and Accra
Kampala and Dakar
Wearing corruption to freedom fests
And Nairobi is Na-robbery Just like
Chicago
And Sao Paolo and Paris:
Skyscrapers leaking urine,
Prosperity throwing sand at eyes of sunlight
for airing nudity
and pubic hair under armpits of truth.

We admit
falling to seductions of a blindness in
appetites Salted fish
hidden behind eyelids
As history ate and we fed on saliva;
Making profits

from broken limbs of humanity feeding a legacy of
indiscipline:
infecting us with that virus
coming to us as cobras
wrapped in flags for hope.
We ate fruit of indiscipline
Leaping on veldts and
forests
Falling as rain into ears
Creeping in cracks between toes
In this dawn of doubt
And pastors turning hunger for salt in faith
unto livestock, rice and maize farms
We call for underground waters of ancestral
winds holding hands in hearts To irrigate
our innovations
across fields of Internet imagination
Refusing to be victims
Throwing jokes at slavery as Jazz,
Glitter in diamonds as Black man's balls
laughing at sunlight
 telling children to rise from drowning;
Dipping indiscipline
into pungent fumes of wet acacia roots
dancing with flames.

Deep in their souls
Smoked fish is wrapped in okro soup
To hide belief in Africa's glide

And sprout into flowering.

They forget yellings
And songs of virgins to lovers
Lost husbands stowed away
by under-water maidens
waving and dancing in swirls on ocean ridges
tossing cloth off loins as ocean rainstorms;
teasing fate of generations.

They know that life wakes up
rolling smiles as dawn; And
babies scream
giving hunger its first cap of dignity:
baby-sitter of life.

They are telling initiates: Shoot
eggs of Architecture out of our
brains and dreams. Let bullets in
borrowed guns rest.
For a chicken with evil wind in its head
runs out
egg-yoke, yellow in its prime,
dripping over its beak her
weapon of murder,
earns getting called a Witch-Hen.;
eater of our tomorrows.

A woman that screams in pain
Cursing her husband

For working in her kitchen;
Sweats as hills and stream
Hold hands with swearing never
again To eat raw honey
Yet failing to pull her ribs tight
For baby in her to honour waiting prayers
of clans,
is mocked with habit and love, often hit by a
husband in sour labour.

Babies are sung to
Of leaders cracking eggs of their old failures:
Wearing bones in their heads
Grown to pillars
Tusks for trapping pencils of Gods'
Drawings of Africa rising from eyelashes
Of mermaids in nameless oceans, Singing
not of revenge;
Rolling out instructions to mould
And build a world on bamboo reeds of justice
Grown in wetlands of love.
The woman who slips out
Wearing dark of night -
Because her man lies cold –
To build a fireplace with a lover
Fears shame for her mother
Wrath of her in-laws
draping her snoring husband with orphanhood.

Her secret lover sends pleas
Into her eyes
For a job near her feet,
Flashing gazes,
Never a boldness of title up his neck..

Girls now tell boys of call in a mission of
Heaven To be bold builders of Africa Crafting
railways across virgin skies:
From top of Mountain Kenya
Top of Elgon and Ruwenzori
With branches to Mountain Cameroun to the west
And Drakensberg in the south:
Sky-trains ever saluting our Ancestors
And guardians watering roots of our imagination.
Never again chasing fire flies
Between legs and earlobes in other geographies;
Turning orphans at dusk unto warriors of laughter
Billowing Africa's ambitions
And inventions of our dawns.

They say with glee: "thirst is Africa, rotting"
We retort: Africa is watching
those picking their teeth,
weaving her laughter Like
time
Shining eyes of History
as lionesses desecrate beauty in Zebras
hyenas gigle over elegant leaps in deers

and pythons slyly hug screaming jackals
in the name of life chewing life Creation
weeding her horizon
Weaving beats and cornrows on dance of landscapes

The rumble of her youth is foretold
 in their stepping
Jumping laughter
 of girls playing cheekying
lighting fires in tempers waving impatience
stoking hope and love in a species

They chant of Lagos and Accra
Kampala and Dakar
Wearing corruption to freedom fests
And Nairobi is Na-robbery Just like
Chicago
And Sao Paolo and Paris
Skyscrapers leaking urine
Prosperity throwing sand at eyes of sunlight
for airing nudity
and pubic hair under armpits of truth.

We admit
falling to seductions of a blindness in
appetites Salted fish
hidden behind eyelids
As history ate and we fed on saliva;
Making profits

from broken limbs of humanity feeding a legacy of
indiscipline:
infecting us with that virus
coming to us as cobras
wrapped in flags for hope.
We ate fruit of indiscipline
Leaping on veldts and
forests
Falling as rain into ears Creeping
in cracks between toes

In this dawn of doubt
And pastors turning hunger for salt in faith
unto livestock, rice and maize farms
We call for underground waters of ancestral
winds holding hands in hearts To irrigate
our innovations
across fields of Internet imagination
Refusing to be victims
Throwing jokes at slavery as Jazz,
Glitter in diamonds as Black man's balls
laughing at sunlight
 telling children to rise from drowning;
Dipping indiscipline
into pungent fumes of wet acacia roots
dancing with flames.

Deep in their souls
Smoked fish wrapped in okro soup

To hide belief in Africa's glide
And sprout into flowering.

They forget yellings
And songs of virgins to lovers
Lost husbands stowed away
by under-water maidens
waving and dancing in swirls on ocean ridges
tossing cloth off loins as ocean rainstorms;
teasing fate of generations.

They know that life wakes up
rolling smiles as dawn; And
babies scream
giving hunger its first cap of dignity:
baby-sitter of life.

They are telling initiates: Shoot
eggs of Architecture out of our
brains and dreams. Let bullets in
borrowed guns rest.
For a chicken with evil wind in its head
runs out
egg-yoke, yellow in its prime,
dripping over its beak her
weapon of murder,
earns getting called a Witch-Hen.;
eater of our tomorrows.

A woman that screams in pain
Cursing her husband
For working in her kitchen;
Sweats as hills and stream
Hold hands with swearing never
again To eat raw honey
Yet failing to pull her ribs tight
For baby in her to honour waiting prayers
of clans,
is mocked with habit and love, often hit by a
husband in sour labour.

Babies are sung to
Of leaders cracking eggs of their old failures:
Wearing bones in their heads
Grown to pillars
Tusks for trapping pencils of Gods'
Drawings of Africa rising from eyelashes
Of mermaids in nameless oceans, Singing
not of revenge;
Rolling out instructions to mould
And build a world on bamboo reeds of justice
Grown in wetlands of love.

The woman who slips out
Wearing dark of night -
Because her man lies cold –
To build a fireplace with a lover
Fears shame for her mother

Wrath of her in-laws
draping her snoring husband with orphanhood.

Her secret lover sends pleas
Into her eyes
For a job near her feet,
Flashing gazes,
Never a boldness of title up his neck..

Girls now tell boys of call in a mission of
Heaven To be bold builders of Africa Crafting
railways across virgin skies:
From top of Mountain Kenya
To of Elgon and Ruwenzori
With branches to Mountain Cameroun to the west
And Drakensberg in the south:
Sky-trains ever saluting our Ancestors
And guardians watering roots of our imagination.
Never again chasing fire flies
Between legs and earlobes in other geographies;
Turning orphans at dusk unto warriors of laughter
Billowing Africa's ambitions
And inventions of our dawns.

WINNIE MHADIKIZELA-MANDELA

I heard their song:
tiny voices wearing freedom soil
inside graves at Dimbaza.
Calls forming clouds
heard my fury
and started floating westward,
dipping little yells on to waves
of the Atlantic Ocean
till shrubs of a beard
caught their chorus
churning them to petals of refusal
to obey devils in carnival of impunities.

The beard twitched;
then convulsed
unto showers of rain:
Belching solidarity
sweat from Africa in veins of Cuba.

Turning and swerving
waves of Caribbean drums on liberation samba
rolled foams across ancient dreams ever bubbling below;
And sung by sharks
to Gods of liberation
fell over Angola in fists of rain
bigger than my punches of AMAANDLAA
over graves at Dimbaza.

Returning baby trekkers of Dimbaza
blew whispers from Angola
across silent sunlights on Cunene River:
Tickling ears of sand dunes of Kalahari
and told of blood-dressed bags
of Christmas gifts for:
Bloodfountain and Feartoria
and Drunkensberg too
Drips of blood to melt plains of ice,
brooding over frozen eggs of holy cruelties
dressed in white collars and hunting rifles.

My Dimbaza trekkers over ocean and veldt
and Kalahari Sands
and Botswana swamps of life,
sung their new Cuban marinda chants
tickling soles under my feet:
Jerking
Folding
Heating bones
Oiling knuckles in my hands,
unto punching chins of Biko
and bald baby Oscar Peterson
and Shaka
And stomping feet of Soweto.

News of Fidel Castro's beard
roasting brave follies in Cubs
on betrayed grasslands along Capricorn's Cape

chased me out of caution's bosom
clad as I was in rags of police bannings
against daring to laugh at a bleeding dusk
as troop carriers dropped
back cold melodies of broken iniquities.

It is not that milk of common motherhood
had silted in my breasts.
Bitter rain soaked
away fear of urinating as I danced
under sunlight
public stares ruling my wits.
Apartheid stole our common right to share shame;
not even allowing us drips of heartdrops
 for healing.

My people have drunk more pain
than sun eating her light by day
 and moon eating her smile by night.
I fear for pain sprouting hate for mothers:
their burden of birth turned to harvest of blame
Blinding glare of freedom
breeding blind revenge as a new moment of power
murdering children and country alike.

My fatigue opens and closes
as stubborn courage watering God's farm;
as fears of surge from a broken walls of an evil dam.

Children learnt to beat their teachers:
not knowing limits of a cry for help.
Those paid with kicks and thuds of batons
replace condemnation with investing
for future dances of drunken muscles.

I know the language of shooting down police bullets
Not strength of fingers for stopping
rumbles of appetite for corruption at dawn.

I must teach women of wooing men
afraid of shadows of memories
in our long season of shooting down humanity.
They must remember geographies
and cheeky wills of their breasts:
Carry their hips
 maps for locations of triumphant futures.
Wrap their heads with traps
for hauling down rays of Divinity.

I will tell them burdens of care for our young lions,
 buffaloes, leopards and elephants;
Tame fingernails of seducers
with spiderwebs for trapping their powers
Honour the MAMA in me in our women
And our Africa.

Even in my solitude of detentions
I dreamed:

of arrows of inventions shooting out to Africa
from atop one thousand hills of Rwanda,
peaks of Kilimanjaro blowing laughter at
Breast Kenya and Breast Elgon
And their Sisters of Ruwenzori and Cameroun
And Atlas
Trading geniuses breaking open cotyledons
Long trained to swim or rot
Inside vaults in village pots
and folklore.

I dreamt of Africa adorning a WRAPPA
of tilled land from Atlantic eyelid on Angola
across Congo's grasslands to lip
of Indian Ocean on Tanzania;
Dissolving brutal hugs of hunger
Irrigating belief in sharing habits of prosperity
Tying garlands of giggles of babies on full stomachs
and light of joy in eyes of mothers
freed from ribs sobbing yet
another umbilical cord torn by graves at Dimbaza.

Of lightening fire bred from Ethiopia's Renaissance Dam
Shaking hands across Africa
with roaring breaths of Hinga Dam
affirming refusal to be washed away by laughing oceans;
Blown away by bellows of mountains

I screamed on a long song of development

from our Cape of New Vision to a blazing lake of Cairo
eating Sahara's stubborn wings;
Rousing waters on Zambezi
Congo
Nile
Niger
And brew fertility in tempers
Roaming on Sahara dunes
Building stable intangibles
waiting in memoirs of our Ancestors
Pregnant with Visions of our new footsteps
across history.
Sharing heart beats of love and futures.

They feared beauty dripped into me
by planting joys of light,
rocking our rotting world with a molten silence.
We shall sing for cooperation
in sharing sunlight
airing romance with moonlight;
Giving back to our Ancestors their gift
to feed our waking seasons:
Showering arrogance in our walk
with our mountaintops....

AGUSTINHO NETO
Five footsteps on
water
dropped black balls of
sweat
on many
geographies:
From eyelashes of
our Atlantic
to Aztecs stares over
Pacific Ocean waves,
sharks sharing
solitudes.

Seeds of silence between skins were planted;
bitter harvests celebrated
gallanted in Villas
Museum and medalled inheritances
Ships rolled on streams Europe's seed of Thirsty Years of
War:
Tribal flowers
Blood plots of sovereignty;
Poisons let out upen the world.

Africa jumped onto their ships
Learning to swim with hands
playing music in chains
beating drums on water bubbles
Rent Jazz melodies to slave ships

Angola poured her soul to Brazil
Bight of Benin rolled away Ibibio to Honduras
Thin Wolof bones dropped in Barbados
And Fulani genes grew roots in Puerto Rico
Mandingo and Lunda fought in Mexico
Rays of Sunlight in our voices
entered cracks on Luanda
Pouring heat over slum pots holding despair:
wise steams in aspirations hissing out
held hands over roofs of neighbours

Our beats in sunlight broke horns
of Europe's poison left in our soils
ocean waves washing back
music of pained farewell from their ships.

We built smokes of liberation
from twigs of wood:
flames fed with songs of women tired
of weeping for victims of greedy ocean waves.
Our war of freedom
broke a leg and four arms,
losing a leg to Mobutu's love for our diamond
shed two arms to Savimbi's soul virus soaked in oil.

Socialism shot fumes of tribalism with a poisoned arrow
mobile bulls' eyes laughing back at us:
Blasting off legs in villages.
American and Chinese ghosts mocked our archery.

Medical science cures patients with patience:
Throwing our hooks soaked in herbal juices
we found fangs of our oil:
its fires flowing in silence
knowing the power of waiting and waiting
in our rage
perfuming our anguish.

Socialism taught us to know footprints of lions:
reading echoes of hunger and old age,
hearing fear of greed
Gluttony in prowls of leopards and crocodiles.
We waved socialism on heat wearing oil,
our proud gait on a stroll.
Women adorned Angolan diamonds;
aroma of oil in hair on heads of men.
We had died long enough to know
H ow to laugh at cockroaches
And chant, without hiccups: 'ALUTA CONTINUA
   VICTORY swims in our genes !
   Carries our History
    Traps rays of
Sunlight in our eyes'.

OFF LIMITS

Staff 1:

Are you seeing what I am seeing? The groin of the other
Excellency is soaked; a large patch, the size of a baby's head.
Fear of other people of power made him wet himself.

Staff 2

The season of incontinence holds power at ages 70 to 94.
With all the farming of sex in our politics, our doctors
recommend insurance against leaking loins from the
"Pinochet virus" when ghosts of murders roam inside
closed eyelids.

Staff 3

In Swaziland power is kept in check by open sunlight on
breasts of virgins; diverting energies away from bashing
political hyenas; and from billions hauled out by gold and
diamond mining wits on seasonless prowls.

Staff 4

All praises to the Nigerian leader who on hearing that
the female national team had won gold had the country
listed as a gold producer; awarding a contract for
earrings for mistresses.

REFLECTIONS OF SPIRIT ORPHAN

As a mushroom he jumped
out, lighting sighs
over treks from debt and termite-eaten homes;
now fowls
scratching to peck worm and seed
 under Florida forest flaps:
 whispering babies to puzzled sleep.

Tear drops
hissed in pools of trembling citizenships
waiting for his word:
Venom dew in a political dawn

Wishing to match Mugabe
at dredging mud red with
Matabele blood:
Cracking history's walls
with staccato of liberation wrath,
His words heralded trampolines
tossing back rivers of Mexican dreams for hope
and eating Fat-Mack and Turkey thighs on stars
They preferred Florida mats of foliage to
tequila on empty bowels.

Mugabe boasted back of Africa's

Ancestors
knowing no rest:
Ever tending clans
weeding history
voices on trampolines thundered: we will never
love on empty stomachs

He said
They said
Mugabe throws up wit
That land in words
 breaking up for sun
and fresh air
 to hug those hungry African mouths
Our trampolines hurl out eggs
painting rot-art on walls
Spilling warmth in Catholic hearts
Inciting roars inside rotting eggs
Seducing alien China
To swirling charity on blue-red pepper:
harvesting tears of ailing America.

Mugabe salutes a China man
for running railways as tattoos on a continent,
her hunters dying in Juba dressed in oil
jackets. Our trampolines throw back spears of
sneer dangles new brave love;
Mocking projects of pity for Africa,
kisses from scramblers

for balls cold on those silent lions
long starved of brutal struggles
of hatred for white skins.

Mugabe sings of Usain Bolt in Rio
Teaching running to millipedes for glee of ancestors;
Thrills in throwing salt into eyes of elephants
reared on Iraqi tears as
Salad cream in animal feed.

Trampolines amuse hearts blue on Cold War gangrene----
--
For regeneration
he vows he shall make police bullets
teach jealousy to thunderbolts in Alabama;
Drop birds on Rasta dreadlocks dead over
Jamaica; Silencing noisy tropical chirpings and
boasts on borrowed guns.

Mugabe hears of flood in Louisiana
reaching hands to Africa's ancestors
Warning
Those who drink water
in clouds over southern Africa
of harvesting sky water full of vengeance
retribution for a season of rights for Black Americans.

Trampoline sees hope in ending
Starvation of mosquitoes by shutting

mouths running on Mugabe
Virus In sterilization of power,
Sent as protein
inoculating mosquitoes with Ebola;
Defending brains of their babies against Communism
in moulding Russian medicine aid pills.

Mugabe says with a hot throat:
Return our sunset
robed in red-in-yellow
given to us by Gods
promising rain
harvests
and cackling and chatting birds.
Cheering over fingers of millet swollen
with tomorrows,
Seeds
promising brewed
nkomboti; And young men
grabbing Handles of hoes
with each giggle in
girls on itch, flowing heat
across their chests;
boys holding futures of
Zimbabwe shooting a horizon
in her eyes at courtships,
as shyness makes fingers
pull or tear leaves of grass,
innocent branches of trees.

We fight for return of our foliage
and wings of mushrooms:
 meeting grounds for romance;
free them from prison behind fences,
 foul habit of Europe's greed,
raw avarice in our tropics
of simple glades of grass.

Trampoline bounces up yells of:
Bring back our hopes
eloped with a billion
kisses in China.
Make our cooking pot sweat again.
Which household takes pride
in food cooked in faraway kitchens
boast of spices grown on
graveyards
flavoured on dead Mandarin bones?

Bring home
echoes of songs
as American women see
babies miss their mouths with
Mama's food pulled from
family grit.

Roars of panic
carrying Jesus

in pots inside eyeballs
blaming hunger
for hate in hearts.
Your Pentecostal Christian fingers
yearn for lynch picnics

Trampoline threw up meat
to crocodiles of fermented barbarism.

www.ingramcontent.com/pod-product-compliance
Lightning Source LLC
Chambersburg PA
CBHW051351150726

48000CB00003B/1131